THE CURSE
OF
THE MUTANT-THING

Published by Dark Titan Publishing.

A division of Dark Titan Entertainment.

Also available in Book.

Mystery of The Mutant-Thing and *Heaven Has Called: All Called From Above*

included in *Tales of the Numinous.*

Also available in paperback, eBook, and hardcover.

Dark Titan Universe is a branch of Dark Titan Entertainment.

First Printing 2021.

Paperback ISBN: 978-1-7366984-7-1
eBook ISBN: 978-1-7366984-8-8

darktitanentertainment.com

WORKS BY TY'RON W. C. ROBINSON II

BOOKS/SHORT STORIES

DARK TITAN UNIVERSE SAGA

MAIN SERIES

Dark Titan Knights
The Resistance Protocol
Tales of the Scattered
Tales of the Numinous
Day of Octagon
Crossbreed
Heaven's Called
The Oranos Imperative

Forthcoming

Underworld
Magicks and Mysticism
The Resistance vs. The Enforcement Order

SPIN-OFFS

In A Glass of Dawn: The Casebook of Travis Vail
Maveth: Bloodsport
The Curse of The Mutant-Thing

Forthcoming

Trail of Vengeance
War of The Thunder Gods
Maveth vs. The Swordman

ONE-SHOTS

Maveth, The Death-Bringer
Mystery of The Mutant-Thing
Shade & Switchblade
Retribution of Cain
The Mythologists
Ambush Bot

COLLECTIONS

Dark Titan Omnibus: Volume 1
Dark Titan Omnibus: Volume 2
Dark Titan One-Shot Collection

THE HAUNTED CITY SAGA

The Legendary Warslinger: The Haunted City I
Battle of Astolat: A Haunted City Prequel (KOBO Exclusive)
Redemption of the Lost: The Haunted City II
Consequences of the Suffering: The Haunted City III (Forthcoming)

SYMBOLUM VENATORES

Symbolum Venatores: The Gabriel Kane Collection
Hod: A Symbolum Venatores Book
Symbolum Venatores: War of The Two Kingdoms
Symbolum Venatores: Elrad's Chronicles
Symbolum Venatores: Mystery of the Magician (Forthcoming)
Symbolum Venatores: Twilight of the Gods (Forthcoming)

A  UNIVERSE SAGA SPINOFF

THE CURSE
OF
THE MUTANT-THING

TY'RON W. C. ROBINSON II

CONTENTS

THE MYSTERY OF THE MUTANT-THING

After a night out of investigating a series of demonic attacks across Washington D.C., Gabriel Abraham, known throughout the world as Abraham The Devil Hunter returns to his workplace called the Revelation Center. Entering his office area as his fellow partners have also went out into investigations themselves. Abraham reads through a series of files laid out on his desk, ranging from poltergeist activity in a suburban area to folkloric figures popping up in many areas throughout the country.

"This is just too much to deal with at one time." Abraham said.

He looks over to another files that is titled, "*The Mystery of The Mutant-Thing*." Grabbing his attention, he opened the file and started reading the information within. He recognized some of the locations that were written down of the Mutant-Thing's possible whereabouts.

"This isn't too far from here."

Turning through the pages of the file, Abraham heard the front door to the building open. He raised his head, looking to see someone inside. Not seeing anyone, he leaves his office and walks out to the lobby area. Unable to find anyone standing around, he returned to his office. Abraham entered his office and seen a man standing behind his desk, reading the files of the Mutant-Thing.

"Who are you?" Abraham said.

The man looked up at Abraham and nodded his head.

"I'm Travis Vail. Some call me the Spirit-Seeker."

Why are you here, Mr. Vail?"

"I am here on the case of the Mutant-Thing mystery and I happened to hear your place was nearby. So, I figured you would have some information regarding the mystery and it appeared to be the truth. This file you have here gives much information."

"If you needed information, you could've went to some other place or even called in to let me know you were coming."

"That's not my style, Abraham. I appear out of nowhere as the wind blows and goes."

Vail placed the file back onto Abraham's desk and walked over toward him.

"For the best, I can ask that the both of us should work together on this mystery in order to discover its truth."

Abraham thought to himself while Vail waited patiently for an answer.

"I can assist you in this mystery, Mr. Vail."

"I appreciate it."

"So, we just go off to this dark wilderness?" Abraham said.

"No. We go to London."

"Why London?"

"I have a friend over there who could give us a helping hand."

Entering London, England at the brink of day, Vail and Abraham walk through London for hours on end with Abraham mostly following Vail around the big city.

"Why are we here exactly?" Abraham said.

"We're here to meet someone who can help us further this mystery. They're in the same field as the both of us."

They approach a Law Firm building and enter it. Inside Vail walked toward the front desk, speaking with the receptionist while Abraham looked around the interior of the room and could sense the small presence of spiritualism around the building.

"Me and a friend are here to see Ms. Cindy Lawson. Is she here right now?"

"Sorry, but she left about an hour ago."

"She did." Vail said. "Thank you anyhow."

Vail walked over the Abraham, seeing him circling his head around the room. Vail tapped him on the shoulder to get his attention.

"I know what you're doing and its best to keep it to yourself for a little while. Until we find out partner here."

"You can feel the spiritualism in this place, and it isn't benevolent energy."

"I am aware of that. Which is why we have to leave this place now."

Leaving the Law Firm, the two walked down the streets of London, passing by the Big Ben. Vail stopped and stared at the tower for a moment. Abraham looked at him and looked at the tower.

"What is it, Vail?"

"Here."

"What about here? What's over here that's important to this case?"

"This is where she will be tonight."

"Who is she?"

"Our helping hand. We'll come back here at nightfall and our partner should be here."

They waited until the night had fallen over London and the moon shined its light brightly above the city. Vail and Abraham returned to the Big Ben with Vail looking upward to the tower, in the far distance, he could see someone standing up atop the tower, looking over the city.

"There she is."

"May I ask who this woman is?"

"Cinderella." Vail chuckled.

"Cinderella? As in the fairy tale Cinderella? Not a possibility."

Vail turned to Abraham with a smirk on his face.

"You hunt demons for a living. I send spirits to the Other Side and you mean to tell me that Cinderella doesn't exist. Yet the world doesn't have any belief in the things we hunt down and eliminate."

"I see your point there. But, how could this be a reality. How did she even get up there in the first place?"

"She has her ways, Abraham. She can tell you more about it than I can."

Up on the ledge of the Big Ben, Cinderella looked around the city of London, monitoring it for any threats lingering that night. She looked down and could see Vail and Abraham standing.

"What is he doing here?" Cinderella said.

She jumped down from the tower, using her coat to glide herself through the air before landing in front of Vail and Abraham.

"I never knew you could do that?" Vail said.

"The coat is made of some materials that allow me to do such a thing."

"I know you're going to ask me why I am here and I will tell you why."

"Tell me then."

"Me and Abraham here need your help on a small case that we're doing together."

"Abraham as in Abraham The Devil Hunter?"

"You've heard of me?"

"The words that surround your hunt for demons goes a long way. Inspires some to become just like you. Others deem you crazy and psychotic for doing such a thing."

"I've been told."

"What is this case that the two of you are working on exactly?"

"The Mystery of The Mutant-Thing." Vail said. "Ever heard of it?"

"I was mentioned once in the office as some kind of teenage joke, but the disappearances of many prove it to be more than just a joke."

"This dark wilderness location exists?" Abraham said.

"It exists. I've been there before on some matters concerning the supernatural."

"Where is this wilderness, Cindy?" Vail asked.

"In Canada. Within the Ontario providence."

"Around some city called Retropolis?"

"That's right."

"Thank you for the information." Abraham said.

"I'm going along with you guys."

"I knew this would happen." Vail said. "That is why I

agreed with it before coming to you."

"Why would you want to come along with us?" Abraham said.

"Because I only know where the wilderness is. Other than that, I know someone who lives around the city who can gives the three of us a better way of handling the area."

"Who is this person?" Vail said.

"Have the both of you ever heard of the Creed of Swords?"

"I've done some studies upon it. Only to know its considered a legend."

"Once during an investigation." Vail said. "Why?"

"Because the help we'll need is a mentor of mine."

They traveled across the Atlantic Ocean heading to Retropolis. Entering the city at the time of night, walking through the city, they see a police car chasing down a pair of criminals through the streets.

"Never been to this place." Vail said. "Is it like this all the time?"

"Pretty much." Cinderella said. "He should be here at any moment now."

"Who will be here?" Abraham asked with curiosity.

They gazed around the streets. From the corner appeared roaming, a black and silver vehicle pass them toward the criminals' car.

"What was that?" Abraham wondered.

"My mentor." Cinderella smiled.

From the car, jumped out The Swordman, dressed in his hooded cloak and Kevlar suit, latched himself onto the top of the criminals' car. Breaking the hood window and pulling the driver out of the car before jumping off the as it rammed itself into a tree near the sidewalk. Cinderella, Vail, and Abraham proceeded to walk toward the scene. Though not with much haste. Yet, they were in a hurry. Stepping closer, they witness The Swordman interrogating the criminal driver as the other one is laid out on the sidewalk. Unconscious from the crash.

"Where is Fear?" The Swordman said.

"I don't know." The criminal said.

"You work for her. You know where she is."

"She never tells us anything. Especially when it concerns locations."

"When you wake up, make sure she knows I'm coming for her."

"What? What do you-"

The Swordman head-butted the criminal, knocking him out. He turned around seeing Cinderella, Vail, and Abraham walking toward him.

"Cindy." The Swordman nodded. "Why are you here?"

"These two men need you help on a case they're solving."

"Travis Vail and Gabriel Abraham."

"How do you know about us?" Vail said.

"I've studied your works. I'm aware of what the two of you do for a living and how much you put into it."

"This is something I never expected to happen." Abraham said.

"Why do you need my help, Vail?"

"We're looking for a place known as the dark wilderness. It's supposed to contain the Mutant-Thing according to its legendary mystery."

"The Mutant-Thing is real."

"You know?" Cinderella asked.

"I've encountered the creature a few times during some of my novice investigations. It's a creature Man should not tamper with."

"We would prefer to see the creature firsthand before we come to our own conclusions." Abraham noted.

"I understand your meaning." The Swordman paused. "Very well, I will lead you to the dark wilderness. If you cannot handle the creature yourselves, I will accompany you."

"What are we waiting for?" Vail said. "Lead the way, Mythological Man."

The Swordman ignored Vail's sayings. "Get in the car."

"What car?" Abraham asked looking around the streets.

From behind The Swordman drove up the *Assassin* or the *Swordmobile* as it's called by the residents of Retropolis. They get into the car, surprise it fits up to four individuals. The Swordman drives off down the streets.

Entering the dark wilderness, The Swordman stood guard, removing his sword out of the sheath. Ready for combat. Cinderella was also prepared to fight if it became necessary. Vail walked through the wilderness, reminiscent of his past time of entering a similar wilderness, encountering an army of druids ranging from adults to children.

"Make sure you're on edge." The Swordman said. "Prepare yourself for anything."

From the trees, something moves past them, rumbling the ground beneath their feet and shaking the trees surrounding them.

"Earthquake?" Abraham said.

"No. It's the creature. It's making itself known."

"That's rather quick." Vail said.

The ground shakes and from beneath it arose the Mutant-Thing. Roaring toward them with anger. The creature was covered in roots, dirt, and grass. The Swordman and Cinderella were prepared to face the creature. Vail and Abraham stood by watching. Vail pulled out his ritual book, staring at The Mutant-Thing.

"Seems the mystery has been solved."

"If the creature makes any move to attack, you send it back into the ground, Vail."

"I will do so, Swordman. Trust me."

The Mutant-Thing roared as it swiped its arms toward Swordman and Cinderella. They moved out of its path quickly to avoid an attack. Swordman jumped above the creature, slashing it with the sword. Cinderella kicked the creature and delivered a small series of blows to its back and chest. Vail raised his hand up in the air.

"I got this." Vail said.

Vail started reading from the ritual book, slowing sending the Mutant-Thing back into the ground. The creature fought back, but Abraham attacked the creature with holy water and chanting words along with Vail. Working together, they send the Mutant-Thing back into the ground and leave the dark wilderness.

The following days, Abraham and Vail continued to meet at the Revelation Center, concerning cases that the two were working on. From the doors entered Papa Afterlife.

"What are you doing here?" Abraham asked.

"I am here on urgent information that concerns the two of you."

"What kind of urgent information?" Vail wondered. "We're listening."

"I have a plan to bring together people such as yourselves to combat a coming malevolent threat that will bring the earth to its very knees."

Vail and Abraham approach Afterlife. They nodded.

"Explain away." Vail gestured.

HEAVEN HAS CALLED: ALL CALLED FROM ABOVE

I

AFTERLIFE VISITOR

Gabriel Abraham turned around in his office, staring at the door. Where Travis Vail, the Spirit-Seeker stood. Vail had his hands in his coat pocket with a stern look on his face. Abraham was confused to Vail's unknown and sudden visit.

"Too soon." Vail said grinning.

"Why are you here?"

"Something's happening, and I can't handle it on my own."

"What do you mean?"

"Something huge. There's a powerful force that's rising beneath the earth. Preparing to make an entrance into our world. One that will certainly end all on this world."

"Demonic force?"

"Stronger."

"Good to see you two here." A voice said, coming from the lobby area of Abraham's Revelation Center.

Vail and Abraham left the office to find the stranger, standing in the lobby. He was of African descent and was dressed modestly. Brown slacks, shoes, with a long-sleeve shirt and vest. He also wore a black fedora. Vail and Abraham have never seen the man before in the fields.

"Who are you?" Vail asked.

"How did you get in?" Abraham questioned.

"Front door was open. Figured I would make myself in and on serious purpose."

"Your name, lad?" Vail said.

"Name stays with me. But, those in our field of work call me Papa Afterlife."

"Papa Afterlife?" Abraham said. "What kind of name is that?"

"Afterlife? As in the magician Papa Afterlife?"

"That would be me."

"Hmm." Vail said. "Funny, you're different that I thought."

"You know this man?"

"No. but, I've heard of his work across the Atlantic. Done some things in Africa, India, places as such."

"Good. Then, you have an idea as to why I'm here."

"Something of the sort."

"Now, what is this thing of serious purpose?"

"There's a dark force coming. Almost near the physical plane of this existence. I was planning on paying you both a visit at your residence. But, given the tow of you here now, makes the message all easier."

"And the message is?"

"This force is ancient. Very ancient. You came across the sin entity during your mission overseas, Vail. You've already sensed the power. Plus, there's a stronger entity roaming around called the Sin Phantom. The Phantom was already chased down by the Death Chaser and is still on the loose."

"Death Chaser?" Abraham said. "There's no such thing as one of them."

"You haven't been studying much have you." Afterlife uttered. "The Death Chaser has been around for ages. You'll need his help in stopping this coming threat."

"You're here to tell us to form a team?" Vail smirked. "Like the heroes over after the Retropolis incident."

"Something along those lines. Because, this threat cannot be stopped with just the two of you. You'll need a unit. One made up of detectives like yourselves, and other forces at work. Spiritual assassins, cryptids, anything you can get to muster up enough power to send this force back into the prison where it belongs."

"And will you be a part of this team?" Abraham asked.

"I'll be watching. An overseer if you so ask."

"Great." Vail said. "Watching from the sidelines."

"I can do more when I'm invisible to the enemy. Soon, you may find that out."

"One can only dream, sunshine."

Afterlife turned away, approaching the door. He stopped, turning back toward Vail and Abraham.

"Unify your members. You do not have much time."

Afterlife exited the Center. Vail turned to Abraham, who was confused about the entire scenario.

"You think Cinderella will be of use to us?"

"We'll have to ask her." Vail said. "Right now, we need to gather some information on possible recruits. If what Afterlife is saying is true, we will need all the help we can get."

II

CALLING THOSE THAT ARE ABOVE

Vail and Abraham set out on their journey to recruit the members possible for their unit. After doing some digging, Vail came up with a list of names. Through much research and sightings across the world, the names he chose were the ones felt closest to the possible unit.

"Where are we headed first?" Abraham asked.

"Chicago. There's a man out there who calls himself the Spiritual Assassin. Figured giving him a look will determine much more."

"His name?"

"John Terror." Vail said. "Supposedly, he's a nubreed."

"One of them. I see."

"Plus, he was in Retropolis during their incident. Means he's in good company with the rising heroes. Maybe he knows more than we do."

Vail and Abraham traveled from D.C. to Chicago. There, they came across a place in the outskirts of the city.

Away from the public. They looked around, it's quiet and still.

"He's here?" Abraham asked.

"Said to be. Might as well knock on the door."

Abraham knocked, the door opened. They didn't see Terror, but they saw his ally.

"Who are you guys?"

"We're detectives." Vail said. "Looking for John Terror. Heard he resides at this place."

"And how would you know that?"

"Like I said, lad, we're detectives."

"Then, you're pretty sloppy." A voice said from behind Vail and Abraham.

"Shit." Abraham said.

They turned around to see terror himself standing behind them with two guns pointed at their heads. Vail smirked while Abraham was unsure of what to do. Terror looked at the young man standing at the door.

"Carl, go inside. You two, follow him."

"Sure thing." Vail said.

They followed Carl into the hideout of Terror. They were placed at the chairs near the working table. Terror approached them, removing his black trench coat and sunglasses. He sat in front of them, measuring them from their size to potential skill set.

"I know what you're doing." Vail uttered.

"Good." Terror replied. "Now, tell me, why are two strange detectives suddenly at my door?"

"We're not ordinary detectives." Abraham said. "We're occult detectives."

"Occult detectives?"

"Yes." Vail said. "He is Gabriel Abraham. Known as the Devilhunter of Washington D.C. You've heard of the Revelation Center, haven't you?"

"Once or twice. And you are?"

"Travis Vail, the Spirit-Seeker. I travel much."

"Ok, so why are you here? Why come to me? And what for?"

"We are recruiting possible members for a team. There's a supernatural threat coming, and it could very well-"

"Not this shit again."

"What?" Vail asked. "What shit?"

"I've done my team shares with those heroes."

"The Retropolis Incident? We know all about it. That tells us, you aligned yourself with those major heroes. Swordman and the like. I have to ask, was this before or after The Swordman confronted the Mutant-thing in the woods?"

"How should I know?"

"Then, how did the two of you meet?"

"We had some similar business. Taking down the same crime lords. We had an early scuffle, but, we're on good terms now."

"Splendid to hear. Then, you don't mind joining yourself with us."

"I'm not a team player. I did what I had to do in Retropolis for those who couldn't defend themselves."

"I get that." Vail said. "But, I have to ask, if the opportunity arose once more, would you take it?"

"Instead of just a city, it's the world." Abraham said. "Much larger than what you're accustomed to."

"How large of a threat are we talking?"

"One that could wipe out all life on this earth and perhaps breach the spiritual planes."

"That bad, huh?"

"It is." Abraham said. "So, what do you say?"

Terror nodded.

"When the time comes, I'll be there."

"How can we be sure of that?" Abraham asked.

"Lend some trust my way. You'll see I'm telling the truth."

"Fair enough." Vail said. "May we leave now?"

"By all means."

Vail and Abraham left Terror's hideout. Returning to Vail's vehicle. They sat inside as Vail looked over the other names. Vail circled Terror's name.

"Who's next?" Abraham asked.

"A friend in London. Figured she would help us out."

"Off to London. Again."

Traveling to London, they waited near the Big Ben once again at night. Abraham looked around for her as he did before.

"She's not here yet?"

"I gave her a phone call." Vail said. "She knows we're here."

Sliding down the walls of Big Ben was Cinderella. She landed, standing in front of the two occult detectives. They hugged each other with smiles. A rare thing to see in their fields.

"I got the call." Cinderella said. "What is it this time?"

"We need your help. Again. Only this time, it involves a more powerful force."

"How powerful?"

"Strong enough to wipe out all life and enter the spiritual dimensions."

"Well, this all sounds like a lot to handle. I'm still in an ongoing investigation."

"If this force rises, you won't have any investigations to cover. Cindy, please, you have to align with us and take out."

"That bad?" Cinderella asked.

"It is."

"Confronting the Mutant-Thing was fun. I guess I can add in the spare time."

"Great." Vail said. "Now, we wait."

"For what?" Abraham asked.

"Cindy wasn't the only one I contacted."

"Who else is in London besides me?"

"An old soul."

From the ground erupted a white mist. Surrounding Vail, Abraham, and Cinderella. The mist turned, morphing into itself, forming an astral body. The body formed and stood before them. Wearing clothing from the Victorian era. The body was of a man. Vail applauded the entrance.

"Abraham, Cindy, meet Robert Shaw. Or as the folktales call him, the Ghost of England."

"The Ghost of England?" Cinderella said. "I thought that was only a story."

"It's more than a story, lass. See, you're looking at him."

"Travis Vail, Spirit-Seeker." Shaw said. "Gabriel Abraham, the Devilhunter. Cindy Lawson, known as Cinderella. I stand before the three of you this night to declare my allegiance to your cause."

"That was easy." Abraham said.

"I figured you may know this we don't." Vail said. "Is there anything we don't know?"

"Best for you to meet with the Unholy Knight called Creed and the Death Chaser, a Soul of Retribution."

"Creed and the Death Chaser?" Cinderella asked.

"Me and Abraham were already told about meeting the Chaser. Trust me, that is soon to come. But, about this Creed fellow, where can we find him?"

"I will guide you to him. But, beware of his aggression. For he is keen to discovering the rising force that threats this world."

"Duly noted." Vail said. "Then, let's get going."

III

THE UNHOLY KNIGHT
AND
THE SOUL OF RETRIBUTION

Returning to the States, Vail, Abraham, and Cinderella are guided by the Ghost of England toward an old church in the Northwest counties. Reaching near the city of Hartford, Connecticut. The Ghost of England signaled a peculiar church building. One with a large black cross standing atop the structure.

"I've been there before." Vail said.

"What for?" Cinderella asked.

"Exorcism of a old man. However, Connecticut is filled with much paranormal and demonic activity. I know from experience."

"And is this where we find this Creed?" Abraham asked Shaw.

"Yes. He will be here soon. Trust my words."

"How soon?" Vail uttered. "I'm just curious is all."

"Soon."

"Tonight? Tomorrow morning? Next week? When? You must have a particular clue."

"You'll see."

"I guess I will."

The Ghost turned to face the group and his eyes shined upon the cross. Yet, he caught movement atop the structure. Vail caught his glimpse and gazed up himself.

"What is it, Trav?" Cinderella asked.

"We've found him. Or, he's found us."

The moving object lunged down toward them, landing on its feet in front of them. They stepped back as the dark blue cloak edged itself back to reveal Creed himself. Creed raised up from his bent position of the landing. Standing tall, facing the unit. His golden eyes gazed at them. His cloak echoing the sound of a chilling wind.

"Who are you?" Creed asked.

"We're detectives." Vail said. "Besides the Ghost here."

"We have no intention of bothering you." Abraham declared. "But, we need your assistance with a dire cause."

"The world is full of causes. Mine aren't sealed in the natural realm."

"Which is why we're here." Vail said. "There's a powerful force rising from beneath the earth. If we don't stop it soon, it will wipe out all life. Everything. Humans. Animals. Plant life. All of it."

"Where is the origin of this threat?"

"I… I don't know."

"Then you are wasting your time."

"Please, listen to us." Vail said, grabbing a hold of Creed's arm.

"Best you remove your hand before you have it no longer."

Vail pulled back his hand from Creed. Smirking.

"You must have some knowledge of a powerful force. Something."

"You speak not of the cryptic Zone."

"Don't think so. I thought that place was sealed."

"It is sealed." Creed said. "I and a fellow angel closed its portals from opening across the world."

"Then, it can't be someone from the Cryptic Zone." Abraham said. "Vail, what do you think it could be?"

"I'm working on it."

From behind them, a spiraling flame emitted from thin air. Causing them to turn around, startling them without haste. Creed stood in front of them, his cloak flowing roughly, his claws sharpened and his gaze keen.

"The hell is that?" Cinderella asked.

"I've seen such a thing before." Vail said.

"Where?" Abraham wondered.

"It's the entrance of the Death Chaser."

The Death Chaser walked out of the spiraling flame and shut its door behind him. He stood face to face with Creed. Two opposing forces of the supernatural realm.

"The Unholy Knight." The Death Chaser said.

"A Soul of Retribution." Creed remarked.

"What's going on here?" Vail asked.

"I should ask you the same, Travis Vail." The Death Chaser said. "I have been tracking all your movements since you were visited by Papa Afterlife."

"Seriously?" Abraham asked.

"Don't feel too bad. It's his job."

"Death Chaser." The Ghost of England said. "Tell us of your purpose here. What do you know of this rising power?"

"More than all of you combined."

"That's good to know." Vail uttered.

"The rising force is a malevolent entity known as Demonticronto. My sworn adversary. Me and my liege were dealing with a soldier of his. A sin phantom."

"Sin Phantom?" Abraham asked. "The hell."

"Don't be too shocked. I know what he's speaking of. I came across this sin phantom during my investigation in Italy. It's a powerful foe. But, a lieutenant demon protected me from its wrath."

"What demon?" The Death Chaser asked.

"Kamagrauto. Heard of him?"

"I have."

"Who is Kamagrauto?" Abraham asked with confusion. "What is going on here?"

"We can explain later, Abraham. For right now, we need to focus on how to stop this Demonticronto demon from rising."

"Creed, Death Chaser." Shaw said. "Align yourselves this day with them. Aid them in stopping Demonticronto and the Sin Phantom."

"I will aid you." Death Chaser said. "Only to stop Demonticronto from causing much harm to this reality."

"As will I." Creed said.

"Excellent." Vail said. "Now, all we need is some guidance on finding a place where Demonticronto's power is growing."

A great flash of white light pierced through he air. Causing a rift between realms. Everyone covered their eyes from the great shine except for Creed and Death Chaser, who are immune to such power. From the rift appeared a man dressed in black with an midnight blue cloak, white gloves and a hat. His long white hair stood out amongst his white facial hair and shining eyes. His pupils could not be seen.

"Who are you supposed to be?" Vail asked.

"I am the Visitant Outlander and I have come to guide you all in this quest you have taken upon yourselves.

IV

THE BROTHERLESS ONE
AND
THE WRATH OF YAH

"Visitant Outlander?" Vail asked. "My, I thought you were just a myth. Hidden away by the ancestors of old."

"I am very real as I stand here before your very eyes."

"I can see that. Which means the other guy exists as well."

"He does."

Vail nodded.

"This is great."

"I don't get what's happening here?" Cinderella asked. "Why have you come to help us? We have Creed and the Death Chaser for that."

"All of you combined together cannot stop Demonticronto's grown power and with the Sin Phantom at his side. I have come to grant an offering to you."

"What kind of offering, lad?"

"To lock away Demonticronto."

"Lock him up?" Abraham asked. "What on earth for?"

"There is no prison that can keep the sin fire from burning Demonticronto." The Death Chaser said. "I will kill him when it comes."

"You shouldn't" Outlander said. "For Demonticronto's existence serves a much greater cause."

"I thought the greater cause was to take him out." Vail said. "Eliminate the evil. Put away the evil. Not imprison it so it can break out."

"Killing such a powerful force will only cause more tragedy than peace."

"And how would you be aware of such causes?" Creed asked. "What happened in the past to alter someone's mind such as yours of a simple cause?"

"I've been around for ages. Much longer than this physical realm. I know what happens when the greater plan is thwarted or tapped."

"Now, I get it." Vail uttered.

"Get what?" Cinderella asked.

"Why the other guy doesn't like Outlander here. He's too into the whole justice motif."

"What other guy?" Abraham wondered.

"He's here." Vail grinned, looking up.

Like a falling cloud, he came down from the night sky. Cloaked in a dark violet cloak and hood. Only his red eyes were visible unto the shining of his presence caused his face to appear. Brighter than Outlander's light. His amulet glowed like the sun. he approached Outlander, standing toe to toe with him.

"Dark Manhunter." Outlander said. "The walking embodiment of the Wrath of Yah."

"Visitant Outlander." Manhunter said. "The Brotherless One. Looking for a way to assist all humanity in its endeavors."

"This is good to hear." Vail said. "Now, we don't need a scuffle between two cosmic forces. Not yet anyway. Manhunter, may I get your view on all of this?"

"Demonticronto must be killed. Execute him before more damage is done."

"Killing him will only bring more harm into this world." Outlander said. "You're speaking tragedy upon their lives."

"Their lives will only find peace when those like Demonticronto and the Sin Phantom are eliminated from existence. Permanently."

"Then, it's settled." Vail said. "We take down Demonticronto."

"As we should." Chaser said. "I will give the final blow."

"Oh, will you and Outlander be joining us on this journey?"

"We will be around." Manhunter said. "Right on time."

"I'll take your word for it."

Manhunter and Outlander vanished from their sight.

Vail looked around, seeing everyone else still standing by. He nodded. Impressed.

"Now, all we need is one more member."

"And who is that going to be?" Cinderella wondered.

"A fellow friend from Retropolis."

"Come on." Cinderella said. "He's not going to stop what he's doing just to help us out."

"I'm not talking about him. I'm speaking of the other guy."

Cinderella thought for the moment. Abraham sighed and Vail grinned.

"Oh. Him."

V

THE MUTANT-THING RISES

The unit traveled to the city of Retropolis. Upon arriving, they noticed the city was under a minor form of martial law. Streets were still and quiet. There was hardly anybody along the sidewalks or outside.

"What's been happening here?" Vail wondered.

"I guess he's cleaning the city faster than I would expect." Cinderella said.

"Hmm." Vail replied.

"Whatever happened to John Terror joining us?" Abraham asked.

"Fumy you mention that. I called him as we were headed this direction. He said he would meet us in the wilderness."

"Meet us there? Why not here?"

"Out in the open I guess."

"We must reach this forest soon." Shaw said. "I can

sense Demonticronto's power surging from below our feet."

"Understood." Vail said.

Entering the dark forest near Retropolis, they traced their steps from before, coming across a large crater-sized hole in the ground.

"This was the spot." Abraham said.

"I remember." Vail replied.

"How do you plan to conjure him?" Cinderella asked.

In the distance, motorcycle sounds entered the forest. They turn back, seeing Terror getting off his bike, walking toward their direction. Vail waved his hands for Terror to see.

"Good thing he's here." Abraham said.

"We'll see for sure."

"I told you I would come on my time."

"Yeah. Right after I called you."

"Seemed like the right moment." Terror grinned. "Now, why are you all out here in the woods? At night?"

"Here to find an old friend." Vail said.

"I wouldn't call him a friend." Abraham gestured.

"Then what is he?"

"A monster." Cinderella said. "One of cryptid origins."

"Nice to know."

Death Chaser started to move around the area. His eyes gazed on the surroundings. As he turned, facing the city. He pointed with great intension. The unit wasn't sure to what he was seeing.

"The Phantom." Chaser said. "He's in the city."

"Are you sure?" Vail asked.

"I know."

"Well, I have an idea." Cinderella said. "Why don't we split up."

"How so?" Abraham questioned.

"Me, Shaw, and the Chaser go find this Sin Phantom while you, Vail, Terror, and Creed summon up the big creature."

"I'm not for this, Cindy." Vail said. "But, since what Chaser said is true, best be going, lass."

Cinderella nodded as she, Shaw, and the Chaser went back into Retropolis. Vail sighed, turning back to the crater in the ground. He stepped into it. Stomping the soil, twisting his foot.

"What are you doing?" Terror asked.

"Waking the big fellow up."

"And he's just going to pop up out of that hole?"

"I hope so. Otherwise, I'm dirtying up my shoes." Vail smirked.

Cinderella, Shaw, and the Chaser walked on he road within Retropolis. Still no one outside. The Chaser moved faster than the two, walking near an alleyway. Cinderella and Shaw followed him. Discovering him coming to a stop, where they saw the Sin Phantom himself.

"You've found me." The Phantom said.

"I'm sending you away." The Chaser said.

"You're not supposed to be here." Cinderella gestured.

"Then, where can I go?"

"To the pit!" Chaser yelled.

Chaser emitted sin fire from his hands and threw it at the Phantom, who dodged the flames. Cinderella ran toward him, trying to grab him by his throat. The Phantom morphed his body into a transparent form, causing Cinderella to slip as he snatched her by the coat and tossed her against the Chaser. Shaw levitated toward the Phantom. Both entities staring down.

"You have violated the natural law." Shaw said.

"And you are going to lecture me on law? I know your history, Robert Shaw. Don't assume yourself as one of the helpless."

"My past is dead. Just as your soul!"

Shaw went to touch the Phantom, but the Phantom grabbed him by his head and his hand glowed like a blue flame above Shaw. He shook himself, trying to get free and as he reached for the Phantom's arm, he was let go.

"Shaw?" Cinderella yelled.

"He's currently occupied right now." Phantom said. "You will have to wake him up."

Shaw's ghostly body arose from the ground, facing Cinderella and the Chaser. The Chaser stepped forward, sensing something odd with Shaw.

"Stand behind me, Cinderella."

"What's wrong?"

"The Phantom, he's done something to Shaw."

"Like mind control?"

"No. he's awoken the once living nature when his

being. Sin has crawled back into his soul. Wickedness is consuming him."

"What can we do?"

"We can beat it out of him. He's only a spirit. Not living flesh."

"Do well with such." The Phantom said. "I must be going. See you all soon when my master arrives!"

The Phantom vanished. Shaw's sin-filled spirit rushed toward the Chaser, grabbing him by the throat and holding him close. Cinderella attended to punch Shaw, but him as a spirit, she was powerless.

"Poor girl." Shaw said. "You're no help once more."

"You leave the woman out of this." The Chaser said. "I will cleanse your spirit of the sin that has entered you!"

"Why? I've never felt more alive."

"You're not alive. You're dead."

Vail, Abraham, Terror, and Creed stood around the crater. Vail reached into his pocket, pulling out his ritual book. Terror was confused, standing amongst a group of men he's never met. He gazed toward Creed, looking at his flowing cloak.

"How does that work?"

"It works with my mind." Creed said.

"Is that so." Terror replied. "I guess it works wonders."

"When it needs be."

"I'm going to read this ritual in Latin." Vail said. "It should summon the big fellow."

"Why Latin?" Terror questioned.

"It works for circumstances like this."

"What of Hebrew, Greek, Arabic, or Persian?"

"I've dabbled in it before. Best be careful with those if you ask me."

Terror nodded. "I see."

"Are you sure this will work properly?" Abraham asked.

"You were with us last time, remember?"

"This isn't like last time. He knows who we are."

"He doesn't know Creed or Johnny boy. We'll be fine."

Abraham shook his head and Vail grinned. Opening the book, turning the pages. He stopped and looked at the three around him.

"Ready?"

"Sure." Abraham said.

"Proceed." Creed said.

"Go for it." Terror gestured. "I'm curious."

Vail stood steady, gazing into the crater. His eyes focused on the page within the book. One hand stretched outward over the crater.

"Voco super te, qui habitas in terra ejus qui creavit elementa. Ergo surge, et sta in conspectu nostro."

The crater began to glow a bright green. They stepped back as the dirt flew into the air, falling upon them like heavy rain. After the dirt had fell and settled, their eyes were focused on who was standing in the middle of the crater. Vail smiled.

"You rose!"

Vail approached the Mutant-Thing. Standing in the

center of the crater. His appearance hadn't' changed since their last encounter. Mutant-Thing looked around, seeing Abraham, Terror, and Creed. He looked down toward Vail.

"Travis Vail." The Mutant-Thing said.

"Listen, bog fellow. We're here on important notice. Not like last time."

"Why have you truly come? Why disturb my slumber?"

"Because there's a powerful force preparing to rise from beneath the earth. If it does, it has the potential to destroy everything."

"What is the destroyer's name?"

"Demonticronto apparently."

"Hmm." Mutant-Thing uttered. "His power is great. He was defeated ages ago by those such as yourselves. But, I see you're missing several warriors"

"They're currently busy finding a sin phantom. Working for Demonticronto it seems."

"And you require my aid in taking Demonticronto down?"

"Yes." Vail said. "That is why we're truly here. Honestly."

Mutant-Thing turned, seeing Creed. He pointed toward him, letting the others look and see.

"He is unholy. Made of malevolent origins. How can he be trusted in such a time?"

"I rebelled against the one who formed me in such manner."

"I smell the stench of the Cryptic Zone on you."

"I was chosen as an apprentice to Adrambadon, Lord of the Cryptic Zone. His demands were dire. But, over time, I broke from his grasp and chosen to make a better change with this curse he has bestowed upon me."

"No matter. He has power over you as long as you're connected to the source."

"Not to cut off this contact." Vail said. "But, we're going to need Creed in order to stop Demonticronto and his little sin lad roaming on about."

"As you say. I will give my aid to this cause. Only to help the earth remain in its current stead."

"Understood." Vail said. "How will this work now? When we find the phantom and Demonticronto, how will you help us? Am I to summon you once more?"

"When the time comes, you will know of my help."

"That's it?" Vail questioned. "A tight, but small riddle."

"Take it for what it's worth, Spirit-Seeker. Now, leave this forest. I must return to my slumber."

"Fair enough."

The Mutant-Thing burrowed himself into the crater as the dirt covered him completely.

"Now what?" Terror asked.

"We find the others. Tell them it's time we come up with a plan."

"Hopefully, they've captured the Sin Phantom first." Abraham said. "Save us all some time."

"Let's find out."

The Chaser and Shaw fought one another with Cinderella giving slight aid to the Chaser. A ring of sinfire had surrounded the sin-corrupted Shaw. Cinderella moved over, standing next to the Chaser.

"You must be purged once more." The Chaser commanded.

"You can't take away such a feeling. I can feel pleasure again. Lust. Greed. I can sense them all."

"That is why I must do this. Only for the purity of your soul."

The Chaser balled up his fist and quickly, the sin fire had rose from the ground, consuming Shaw. The others arrived as they saw Shaw within the flames and chaser with Cinderella standing back.

"The hell's going on?!" Vail yelled.

"The Sin Phantom planted a seed within Shaw's mind. He became consumed with sin. I am purging it from his spirit form."

"Is he still in there?" Abraham asked.

"Yes." Cinderella said. "Chaser is burning the sin seed out of him."

Shaw continued to burn, and the Chaser opened his hand, ceasing the spiral sin fire as it returned to the ground, only leaving Shaw's spirit remaining. They ran over toward him. Chaser placed his hand upon Shaw's head.

"How is he?" Cinderella asked.

"He's still in there. The sin is gone."

"Just like that, you burned it out of him?" Terror asked.

"Yes. This is my line of work."

"Would be nice to have all humans enter this treatment."

"It would kill them." The Chaser said. "They're still in their mortal forms. The human body cannot handle such pain from sinfire."

Shaw's eyes opened as he arose from the ground, looking at his body.

"You purged it from me."

"As I only could."

"Now, since that's out of the way, we need to make a plan and quickly." Vail said. "I fear Demonticronto's is not as far away as we assume."

"He isn't." The Chaser said.

"And how are you aware of his whereabouts?" Abraham asked.

"I can sense him. He's walking upon the earth right now and he isn't far from our location."

"Then, you can track him."

"I can."

"Then, let's get going." Vail uttered.

VI

THEY HAVE BEEN CALLED

The unit followed the Chaser out of Retropolis and have stumbled upon a cemetery near the United States border. The cemetery was calm, quiet, and still. Vail shrugged his shoulders walking past the headstones on the ground.

"What is it now?" Cinderella asked Chaser.

"He's here." Chaser said. "He is here."

"Where?" Vail wondered. "Is he under the ground or standing in front of us? Just invisible?"

Dirt kicked up from a grave as the Sin Phantom made himself known once more. The unit stood their ground toward the Phantom, who did not move past the gravesite.

"You've come." The Phantom said.

"No shit, lad." Vail replied. "You know why we're here."

"I do, and he is proud to have you here. To bear witness to his uprising."

"Then, where is the bastard?"

"Where's Demonti?!" The Chaser yelled.

"He's right here."

He grave turned into molten lava within seconds and created an opening in the ground, a deep pit. The Phantom moved from the grave as lava flew up in the air, yet, not falling back toward the ground.

"You see what I'm seeing?" Vail asked Cinderella.

"Yeah. I do."

Within the lava, the unit could see something moving. Hovering within the lava. As the lava settled its pouring, the figure could be seen. His red-skin, torn tunic, and long fiery hair. He landed on his feet beside the Phantom.

"There you are!" The Chaser said.

"Yes. I am here."

"Demonticronto I presume." Abraham gestured.

"In the flesh as they say."

"You've come to the wrong place, fellow."

"Oh, have I?"

"We're sending you back into your prison." Abraham said.

"I give you the opportunity to try."

The Chaser grunted, running toward Demonticronto with his arms covered in sin fire. The Chaser went for an attack but speared to the ground by the Phantom with a quickening force.

"You and I have a score to settle, Retributor."

"You've forgotten me." Shaw said, tackling the

Phantom.

The unit began their battle with Demonticronto. Creed went for the aerial attack as Demonti's height was near thirteen feet tall. Demonti's strength from his arms, knocked Creed from the air, as well as his dragon-like tail, swiping Vail, Abraham, and Cinderella off their feet.

"This is depressionaly easy." Demonti grinned.

"*'Depressionaly*?" Cinderella said. "Is that a word?"

"Doesn't matter." Vail said. "We're not here to learn new words."

Vail chanted out a binding spell, causing the air around Demonti to constrict him. Holding him steady while Creed attacked him from his head to his torso. Abraham also chanted a spell to keep Demonticronto still. Meanwhile, the Chaser and Sin Phantom battled it out through the cemetery. Chaser snatched Phantom by his neck and tossed him against a headstone. Phantom dodged an incoming punch from Chaser with sinfire dripping from his fist. Shaw went for an attack of his own yet tripped by the Phantom.

"This is sad for your kind." Demonticronto said. "I assumed humanity had learned the means of working with such magic feats."

Demonti increased his strength, breaking the spiritual bonds around him, knocking down Vail, Cinderella, and Abraham. He grabbed Creed's cloak and slammed him into the ground. Terror ran up, firing shots with his pistols. Demonti grabbed the pistols, slapping Terror with them and stomping on his back. Demonticronto savored the moment.

"You're no match for me. I am above such primitive feats."

"I've heard that before." Cinderella said.

"Haven't we all."

The sky quickly opened above the cemetery and from there, Visitant Outlander and Dark Manhunter appeared before them. Standing in front of Demonticronto. He moved from the downed team and stepped forward to Outlander and Manhunter.

"The two of you, working as one? Impressive."

"Don't take this lightly, demon." Manhunter said.

"You have trespassed upon a realm you have no authority."

"Spare the reasoning, Eidolon. I have come for my purpose only."

"And your purpose shall be?"

"To rule over Man. As the others should have done eons ago."

"That is where you're wrong." Manhunter said, raising his hand.

"You cannot end me." Demonti said. "I am still needed. I know the end of all this. I am not a fool."

"Yet, you know the end and continue to act as such." Outlander said. "No, we will send you back to your realm until the opportune time arises according to the Word. However, this team of outcasts have revealed they're just as a match for you when the time comes."

"Look at them! They're not a match for me!"

"So, you truly do not know the end of all things." Manhunter said. "Go home, demon."

Manhunter conjured up a portal beneath Demonti's feet and he fell into the deep lighted pit. The Phantom also was pulled from the Chaser's grasp and dragged into the pit. Once they were inside, the pit closed at the command of Manhunter. Then, the area was still once more. The unit returned to their feet, approaching the embodiments of justice and vengeance.

"I'm confused." Vail said. "What's happened here?"

"Demonti knows of his end." Outlander said. "This day was not such."

"The end?" The Chaser uttered. "I know his end for I have seen it."

"You have, Soul of Retribution." Manhunter said. "But, this is not the day."

"Hold on." Vail said. "When is this end you're speaking of?"

"Soon." Outlander said. "Sooner than the world will know. For the end is near and it is right at the door."

"As in the days of Noah and such like?"

"You know the details, Spirit-Seeker." Manhunter said. "For a dark force will return to this world and claim it as his own. Many will fall at his feet in opposition and will rise once more. For now, continue as such and you will succeed."

"Fair enough."

"Best you all go your own ways." Outlander said. "Demonti will not return quickly as you will imagine. For there are other threats that pose damage to this world and the realms. When the time comes, you all will be united once more. For you all are *Heaven's Called*."

"Yet, you will not know the day, the time, nor the hour." Manhunter said. "We bid your farewell. For now."

Outlander and Manhunter disappeared from their sights. Vail looked back at everyone and chuckled.

"Well, shit."

Afterwards, they each returned to their domains. Creed and Death Chaser continued their spiritual work, Cinderella and Shaw returned to London, Abraham made it back to the Revelation Center in D.C. and Vail continued his work across the world. Yet, somewhere secretly, a stash of grimoires had been taken by an unknown group. A group led by a priest who has a past with Vail.

THE CURSE OF THE MUTANT-THING

I

<u>DETECTION OF THE ELEMENTS</u>

With Demonticronto defeated, the newly formed team of Travis Vail, Gabriel Abraham, Cinderella, Creed, Death Chaser, John Terror, Ghost of England, Visitant Outlander, and Dark Manhunter head their separate ways. Amongst them in the battle was the Mutant-Thing, whom left the area, returning to its own estate deep into the wilderness. While mediating, the Mutant-Thing sensed something sinister and it made its move east, toward the border of Manitoba.

Sometime later, a series of strange murders were committed within and outside the city of Winnipeg. Entering Winnipeg are two detectives. Keen in their skills. Detectives Cole Yeager and Lewis Knight enter the police station to learn more about the murders. Greeting the two is Chief Bill Thompson, who walked them to his office.

"Good to have you guys here." Thompson said.

"We got the call and figured it was something worth doing." Lewis replied. "Now, what is truly going on?"

"Where to start? Ah, we've been receiving several

reports of bodies being found out in the woods. Apparently, they add up to a series of murders. Are they committed by the same suspect? We don't know and that's why you two were called up."

"Wait a second." Cole jumped in. "You called us here to find the suspect? Without any evidence to the case?"

"Only evidence we have are the bodies in the woods."

"How many bodies are we talking?" Cole wondered.

"A dozen. Maybe more."

"Ah shit." Lewis said. "Sorry, I wasn't sure it was that many. Thought it might've been five or six at the most."

"Who's at the sight now?" Cole asked.

"A few of our patrolmen. Keeping the place secure from prying eyes. You know how people are these days. Always filming something for social media."

"Generational things." Lewis scoffed. "They come and go."

"One more thing I must ask." Cole said.

"Speak it."

"How come you didn't call one of those 'risen heroes' to solve this case?"

"We don't have no heroes in Winnipeg."

"I see."

"Anyway, while you two deal with the case on the outside, we have a reporter who's already on the case speaking with possible witnesses."

"A reporter for what?" Cole questioned. "Lewis and I can talk with the witnesses."

"I agree to that." Lewis said. "Why bring in someone else when we're already here?"

"To broaden out the case. She will go around and question those who may have some insights to the murders.

Be it family members of the deceased or those who might have seen something strange these past several days. You'll probably bump into her on your way around the city or when you return back here."

Yeager nodded, standing up from his seat and walking toward the door. Knight turned to him and looked over to the Chief. The Chief only pointed at the door to which Knight shrugged his shoulders with a nod, standing up and walking out of the office with Yeager.

"You could've said you wanted to head out now." Lewis said.

"I went to the door." Cole replied. "What other signal is there to add on?"

Traveling out near the wilderness of Winnipeg, Cole and Lewis stepped out of their vehicle, seeing several officers surrounding a pile. From their perspective, the pile appeared to be only mounted trash. Until they walked closer and saw arms and legs covered in mud and blood. Lewis covered his nose without hesitation while Cole continued walking closer. No expression showed or appeared. Cole was collected as he stepped toward the officer.

"You guys must be the ones they talked about."

"We are." Cole said. "We'll take it from here."

The officer nodded and stepped away as Cole kneeled toward the bodies. Their stench strong as Lewis knelt down as well, covering his face with a cloth. His eyes went in several directions. Both from the bodies and toward Cole. His eyes locked in on Cole for a second as he shook his head.

"This smell ain't bothering you or something, eh?"

"No. The smell does not command my body to respond to its own concerns."

"The hell that's supposed to mean?"

"Means I have ultimate control over my body than the bodies we see in front of us."

Lewis scoffed.

"Oh, good for you."

Cole searched through the bodies, seeing arms and legs of men and women. Cole leaned in closer and caught a glimpse of fur. Confused, Cole stood up and walked toward one of the nearby trees, looking down on the ground as he picked up a stick. He returned to the pile, using the stick to move the bodies.

"What are you doing?" Lewis wondered. "Cole, what's the stick for?"

"There's something else here. Something other than people."

Using the stick, Cole moved the bodies, uncovering a smaller pile of dead animals. Lewis stepped back, covering his face even more as Cole leaned in further. Looking at the animals, Cole nodded.

"Elk." Cole said. "Looks like some beavers as well."

"The hell's happening out here?" Lewis said.

"We're dealing with something that shares no discrimination between human and animal. This thing kills whatever it desires."

"What kind of person does this." Lewis replied.

"I don't think it was human." Cole added. "Something else."

II

<u>LAW OF NATURE</u>

A young woman stepped outside of her car in front of a home which appeared to be separate from the nearby suburban area. The woman carried a journal as she approached the front door and knocked. She waited and the door opened, revealing a woman similar to her age. She glanced at the woman and the journal.

"Who are you?"

"I'm Cassandra Day. I'm here to speak with you concerning the murders."

"And why would you speak to me about murders?"

"I was informed you might know what's happening here. What may have caused them."

The woman went silent. Her eyes moved left and right before she sighed, allowing Cassandra to enter her home. Once Cassandra had entered, the woman took a quick glance around the front of the home before shutting the door. The woman led Cassandra to her dining room table, where Cassandra sat down. The woman walked over to her coffee pot, pouring a cup.

"You want a cup?" She asked.

"No thank you." Cassandra replied. "I'm well."

The woman picked up her cup and sat down next to

Cassandra.

"I never got your name." Cassandra said.

"My name's Morhana."

"Morhana." Cassandra said. "That's an intriguing name."

"It's foreign in many parts."

"Forgive me, but, that name sounds like it would belong to a witch."

"I am a witch."

"Oh." Cassandra paused.

"No need to be afraid. I'm not a sinister one."

"Well, I'm here to see if you may know what's been happening here."

"Regarding the murders?"

"Yes."

"I will tell you for starters, the cause of these murders are not only natural. They are also the cause of a supernatural force."

"A supernatural force?"

"You can't believe all of those murders were caused by a simple serial killer."

"There's records of it occurring in many places."

'Is that right?"

"Yes." Cassandra said. "I've been across this country and a few others to realize that murders such as this have happened before."

"Did you ever find the cause of the murders? The suspect?"

"Only for a few."

"What of the others?"

"The suspect remains a mystery."

"To the natural eyes."

Cassandra sighed, writing in her journal. Morhana raised herself up in the chair to get a glance. Cassandra spotted Morhana's movements, glancing at her from the journal.

"Just curious as to what you're writing."

"I'm writing what I need to solve this mystery."

"And I guess I'm a helper to your cause?"

"A minor one at the moment."

"Still good enough."

"Quick question." Cassandra said. "Your witchy tactics? How did you become one?"

"I was born this way."

"You were born a witch?"

"I was born into a coven. My mother was a witch as was my grandmother. They taught me the ways of sorcery and one I was of age, I was welcomed into the coven with open arms."

"Where is this coven now?"

"Underground. Although, we move around in the open secretly."

"How come?"

"Because, there are forces out there who seek to rid the earth of my kind."

"Let me guess. Witch hunters?"

"More than hunters. Sorcerers. Spiritual forces."

"And how do you face them?"

"By using what I've learned in my youth. They primarily use magic as their resource of power and I use it against them."

Cassandra closed the journal. Morhana's gaze was set on the journal.

"So, if I were to go by what you've said, I should be

searching for the supernatural element to this case?"

"That would be your best bet."

"And what if you're wrong?"

"I'm never wrong." Morhana scoffed.

Cassandra nodded as she stood up from the table, grabbing her journal.

"Thank you for your time."

"No. Thank you."

Elsewhere, Cole and Lewis travel to a laboratory in the areas of Winnipeg. After gaining information from the officers and forensics, they make their way to speak with a scientist who may have some details concerning the suspect to the murders. Lewis parked the car in front of the laboratory and Cole stared. Lewis noticed Cole's silence and his stillness. Looking back between Cole and the lab.

"What's the issue?" Lewis asked.

"Something's not right about this place."

"Where are you getting this from? The door or the surroundings?"

"Both."

"Look, let's just go in there, speak with this guy to see what he knows, and we'll be out of this place before the sun sets."

"I know." Cole said.

"You know."

"I know."

The detectives enter the laboratory and quickly, they get the glimpse at the scientist who's operating at such a quick speed. Moving back and forth between desks. Lewis looked at the scientist's attire and scoffed.

"He sure dresses the part."

"The part?" Cole questioned.

"You know. The white coat, glasses. The whole gear set."

"Ah." Cole sighed.

Cole stepped forward, knocking on the desk nearby. The scientist jolted, turning around to see the detectives. He glanced toward them, looking at their attire. He raised his finger, pointing at them in a frantic fashion.

"Are you two students?"

"No." Lewis answered. "We're not students. We're detectives."

"Oh. But why would detectives be here in my lab on this day?"

"To ask you some questions concerning the murders." Cole replied.

"The murders? What murders?"

"You aren't aware of the murders in this city?" Lewis wondered.

"I'm afraid not."

"The hell you've been this whole time." Lewis asked. "Stuck in this lab or something?"

"What my partner is trying to say is how do you not know?"

"I keep to myself. Mostly."

"What's your name by the way?" Lewis asked.

"I'm Dr. Larry Grint."

"Grint?" Lewis said. "What kind of name is that?"

"A unique one."

"Sounds like one." Cole added.

Grint turned back toward his desk, Cole stepped forward looking atop the table, seeing nothing but papers and folders. Lewis looked around the lab, nothing interest him nor gave any indication that Grint may know something. Lewis shrugged his shoulders.

"I think we hit a dead end."

"You're certain?" Cole asked.

"I am. The guy's not giving us anything. Hell, he's not even paying attention to us."

"Oh. I almost forgot!" Grint yelled.

"And that is?!" Lewis asked loudly.

"I saw trails leading into the woods several days ago. I wasn't sure what is what or where it came from."

"Trails of what?" Cole asked. "What were the trails made of?"

"It looked red. Like a bright red."

"You're talking about blood?" Lewis said.

"I assume so. Because the trail led to the pile of bodies."

Cole turned toward Lewis, a still expression. Lewis only let out a sigh and shook his head, turning toward the exit.

"Anything else?" Lewis asked, rubbing his eyes.

"Nothing so far."

"There is it." Lewis turned away.

"Thank you for your time." Cole said.

"Sure thing, gentlemen."

Lewis and Cole exit the lab and stand on the sidewalk next to their car. Lewis placed his hands on his side, shaking his head while gazing down. Cole was still. No expression. He turned toward Lewis.

"What now?"

"Let's give the site another glance."

"A glance for what?" Cole wondered.

"Humor me this once."

The detectives returned to the body site to find more details. Upon arriving, they discover they're the only ones there. The officers who were previously in place around the site were gone as were the forensic scientists. Lewis began to worry and Cole only walked closer to the bodies. Lewis, feeling uneasy placed his hand over his holster.

"Something off about this place." Cole said.

"You're just now realizing it." Lewis answered.

"No. I mean there's someone else here."

Lewis looked around. Only seeing the trees and the road. He tossed his arms in the air.

"I don't see anyone out here besides you and me."

"Not a human being." Cole said. "Something else."

Cole stared into the wilderness, Lewis could see Cole was focused on something. As he turned toward the tress, he saw what Cole was staring at. A tall figure, shrouded in the shadows of the trees. Yet, the figure stood over nine feet in height as its presence brought sheer terror over Lewis. Cole's eyes were set on the figure as Lewis went for his gun, raising it up toward the figure.

"The hell is that?!" Lewis yelled.

"Don't shoot!" Cole screamed. "We're not sure why it's here yet."

The figure did not move nor make any noise. It only stood still, staring at the two detectives. Lewis was shaking as his hands began to sweat. Cole kept Lewis calm as he stepped forward toward the woods.

"The hell are you doing?!"

"Trying to get a better look."

"You see how tall that son of a bitch is?!"

"I do and I'm not concerned."

"Cole! Get your ass back over here!"

"Just calm down, Lewis." Cole responded. "I got this."

"You don't got shit!"

Cole had stepped close enough to reach the trees and he stood still. He raised his head to get a better look at the figure and what he saw he couldn't understand. Looking into the figure's eyes, Cole nodded and began to step back slowly. Lewis watched on as Cole returned toward him and only nodded at the forest. Lewis looked at Cole and turned back toward the trees, seeing the figure had vanished.

"The hell'd it go?"

"Deep into the forest." Cole said.

"How do you know?"

"It's hard to explain."

"The ride back to the station is long enough for you to explain."

Cole sighed, opening the car door.

"Hope you'll comprehend."

"Comprehend what?"

They left the site, returning to the base. Once they entered, everyone inside could hear Lewis ranting on about the incident. Lewis continually screamed toward Cole and Cole stayed silent as they entered the Chief's office. The Chief saw the commotion, standing up from his desk.

"What's this all about?"

"We went back to get a better look." Lewis said. "For more information. Little did we know we were being watched."

"Watched? By who?"

"Not a who. A what."

"Some... thing." Lewis answered. "It was strange."

"Cole, what's he talking about?"

"We went back to the body site after our visit with Dr. Grint."

"You spoke to Dr. Grint?"

"Yes sir."

"And what did he say about the murders?"

"Hardly a damn thing." Lewis responded. "the guy's a crackpot. He wasn't even giving us attention. Just busy with whatever the hell he was doing inside that lab."

"And the stalker in the woods?"

"It wasn't human." Cole said.

"What's that supposed to mean?" The Chief questioned. "What do you mean by 'not human'?"

"The thing was tall." Lewis said. "Had to have been over nine-feet at least."

"Is this true, Cole?"

"It is. I got a closer look."

"Yeah. This jackass decided to step forward near the thing. Go ahead, Cole. Tell him what you saw."

Cole sighed.

"I saw the figure in its full form. Its body was made of bark. Leaves growing from its limbs. It carried the stench of dew and its eyes were bright like the sun. It didn't speak, but it communicated in my mind. Like it spoke to me true some kind of brain wave."

"You talking psychic stuff?" the Chief asked.

"I am."

"Well, I guess I'll break it to you guys. I've heard of this being before."

"You have?" Lewis asked. "Seriously?"

"Yes. I only thought it was just some kind of joke to scare away tourists or to attract tourists. Either way, it gained some attention several months ago.”

“What is the thing?” Cole asked.

“Some of the locals call it the Environment Man.”

“Environment Man?” Lewis said. “Like a man who monitors the environment?”

“Not a man. A spirit. A ghost. Whatever it is, it’s not human nor was it born human. The legends state the Environment Man was created and designed to watch over the environment at all cost. No matter the location or the scenario. Some incidents recall the being always present near deceased animals or humans. The fact that you two saw it at the body site only confirms there’s something strange going on in this city and we need to get to the bottom of it.”

“I agree to that.” Lewis replied. “But, what are we going to do next? The doctor was a dead-end. Where’s that reporter you spoke of?”

“She already made her rounds. She spoke with a witch apparently.”

“No shit?” Cole said. “Does she know about the Environment Man?”

“Who’s to say. But the witch told her there’s something supernatural involved with the murders. So, if that’s enough to go on.”

“This shit is getting weird.” Lewis said. “Definitely for me.”

“Well, you can start at another site.”

“Another pile?” Cole asked.

“Not exactly. The site is presumed to be a residence for the culprit. Perhaps, the murderer left something behind. I’ll let the two of you head out there to find out.”

The Chief handed them a map and on it was the

detailed location of the second site. Lewis nodded, wiping the sweat from his forehead as Cole folded the map, putting it in his pocket.

"We'll come back with the details." Cole said.

"I'm sure you will. Also, be on the lookout just in case you run into him again."

"We will." Lewis said. "Armed up this time."

III

EVERYTHING HAS A SEASON

Cole and Lewis made the drive up to the secondary site. They see the location and the ruins. Lewis shrugged his shoulders, turning to Cole. He pointed toward the building.

"Is this what I believe it to be?"

"Another lab." Cole answered.

"You're sure this is the spot?"

"I'm sure. Chief marked it on the map clearly."

Lewis stepped forward near the laboratory door. Seeing a padlock, he sighed.

"Someone wanted to keep this place shut."

"And who do you have in mind?" Cole asked.

"A crazy scientist. As always."

Cole pulled the lock as Lewis took a gaze around the area.

"Would be better if we had the key."

Lewis' attention quickly turned toward the tree line behind the lab. Cole looked on, hearing some rustling. Lewis reached for his gun with speed, aiming it toward the woods.

"Something's watching us again."

"It's not the Environment Man." Cole said.

"How do you know? You see him?"

"No. Because the rustling is multiplied."

"Meaning?"

"There's more than one person in those trees staring at us."

From the trees walked out over a dozen figures. Shrouded in black robes and hoods. They stepped forward slowly toward the detectives. Lewis yelled, holding his gun steady. Cole only glared, slowly going for his weapon.

"The hell's going on in this city?!" Lewis screamed.

"Who are these people?"

"How should I know!"

"Their apparel." Cole noticed. "They look to be part of some group."

"More like a cult if you ask me!"

The hooded one moved toward the detectives, their arms stretched out. The fingers shaking as they reached closer. Lewis kicked one in the chest and backed up. Cole only moved away from them. It reached the point where the two were backed up against their vehicle as the hooded ones circled them. Corning them in full. Lewis shook his head with the gun in hand. He was ready to fire. Cole only shut his eyes and raised his head.

"What are you doing?" Lewis asked. "Praying?"

"You could say that."

Once the hooded ones had their hands on the detectives. Lewis screamed and fired a shot, killing one of the hooded ones. The death didn't not shake them nor stop them. They kept coming. Lewis went for another shout, however, the ground began to quake. Cole's eyes open as he looked toward the trees. The hooded ones ceased, turning around to the woods. What they saw was a large crack emerging from the ground, separating the grassy plain from the concrete ground of the driveway. The crack stopped directly at the feet of the hooded ones. They glared down at the crack as Lewis and Cole slowly stepped back. The ground shattered open as the detectives saw the mutant-Thing attack the hooded ones. Snatching them by their heads and tossing them into the woods. The hooded ones all went in for the attack. Circling the Mutant-Thing, climbing him due to his immense height. Lewis looked on, seeing the Mutant-Thing was as tall or taller than the Environment Man.

"That's not the Environment Man." Lewis realized.

"It's something else." Cole said.

The Mutant-Thing exploded himself, impaling the hooded ones through their heads and chests. Their bodies dropped to the ground as the Mutant-Thing glared toward the detectives. Lewis slowly lowed his gun and Cole only stared.

"What is that?" Lewis wondered.

"Something beyond our understanding."

The Mutant-Thing nodded and turned back, bellowing into the crack and it closed itself as the Mutant-Thing disappeared. Lewis looked down, noticing the crack was gone.

"The fuck's going on here?"

Elsewhere, Cassandra made her next stop at Dr. Grint's lab. Surprisingly, Grint allowed her inside his lab. While there, Cassandra questioned him on the recent findings involving the bodies. Grint laughed, confusing Cassandra.

"You know, some detectives were here earlier. They

asked me about the same thing."

"Did you tell them anything?"

"Not much."

"Why not? You're not aware of it?"

"I am aware. However, it is not any of my business."

"But, you live here. What happens here must certainly be on your mind when you're out in the public."

"One would believe such. Yet, it is better to keep your mind on your own affairs. Leave the others to their own concerns. Otherwise, you might cause trouble that shouldn't never have been."

"Well, I'll ask you this one question. What are you working on?"

"Ah. Something which will be used in the near future."

"For what purpose?"

"To make Winnipeg better. The environment better. Hopefully, once it's revealed, the countries of the world will accept it and my work will be spread across the world."

"You want to make the world a better place?"

"Doesn't everyone to some extent."

Cassandra nodded, putting her journal into her bag.

"So, you're not aware of anything. No strange sightings of any kind?"

"Nope."

"Thank you for allowing me to speak to you."

"Same to you, madam."

Cassandra had left the lab with Grint continuing with his work just as he did with Cole and Lewis. Back at the department, another detective had arrived after a call with Chief Thompson. She walked in and went straight for the Chief's office. She knocked on the door to get his attention and as he saw her he welcomed her inside the office.

"Go you've made it, Detective Salvatore."

"You called. Said something major was happening and I couldn't miss it."

"Yana, what's happening here, will need as much attention as possible."

"Where do I start?"

IV

<u>NEW FACES</u>

Cole and Lewis returned to the office. Walking through the lobby toward the chief's office, they stop and see the new detective in the interrogation room with a suspect. Lewis confused, pointed while gazing at the other officers passing by in the lobby.

"Who's she?"

"That's not the reporter." Cole answered.

"You're sure?"

"I'm positive."

Lewis shook his head and waved his hand.

"I'll ask the chief."

"By all means. Oh, you're going to tell him of what we saw out there?"

"Which part? The druids or the monster from the ground?"

"Better to tell both."

Lewis sighed as he entered the office. While Lewis spoke with the chief, Cole watched Detective Yana interrogate the suspect. The suspect in general appeared as a mid-sized man. Cole watched his movement as Yana spoke more questions. The thing which fascinated Cole was the calculator sitting on the table. Why a calculator instead of a

Smartphone Cole wondered. However, he approached the door and opened it. Yana turned around, seeing Cole.

"I'm sorry to interrupt." Cole said. "Me and my partner didn't know there was another detective here on similar work."

"I'm Yana." She extended her hand. "Yana Salvatore. I come from a town nearby."

Cole shook her hand with a nod.

"Nearby. Are you here to help with the murder investigation?"

"I am. Which is why I'm questioning this man."

Cole turned toward the man, seeing the calculator up close and the man's apparel. Which was only red buttoned shirt and black slacks. His hair was medium length, passing his ears and his facial hair was kempt to a degree. Cole pointed at the calculator.

"Don't have a phone?"

"I do. But, the calculator has given me much freedom."

"Noted."

"This man is Waid Givens. Calls himself the Calculator Man."

Cole stared. His eyes going back and forth between Yana and Waid.

"Calculator Man?"

That's what he said." Yana said. "He seems to know something greatly about the investigation."

"Knowing what?"

"He states he calculated the true suspect."

"Calculated?" Cole asked. "With the calculator?"

Yana sighed.

"Yes."

"And where do we go to find this suspect?" Cole asked

Waid.

"You don't know?"

"How can I? You're the one with the answers today."

"My calculator estimated the suspect is always centered around the cemetery."

"Cemetery?" Yana said.

"What cemetery?" Cole asked.

"The one where the eeriness is always welcomed."

"Huh?" Yana said. "What's that supposed to mean?"

"It means the environment feels very, very strange. Like beyond this world. Beyond nature."

"How can we take this for face value?"

"You can't. Only you can estimate the numbers to calculate the location."

Cole took a moment of thought. He nodded.

"I'll track down which cemetery presents this eeriness you're talking about."

"Are you going out there?" Yana asked.

"Me and my partner will head on out there. It's what we do mostly."

Cole exited the room and as he shut the door, Lewis approached him from the chief's office. Lewis wiped his forehead and took a moment to breathe.

"What happened in there?"

"What happened in there?" Lewis said, pointing at the interrogation room. "You spoke with the new detective?"

"I did."

"And the suspect in there?"

"Waid Givens. He calls himself the Calculator Man."

Lewis stared.

"The fuck's that?"

"I don't know."

"He calls himself the Calculator Man? Seriously."

"Yes, he does."

"This case is getting stranger by the hours. How long do we have to keep this going?"

"Right now, we focus on getting it done. Now, he said he knows the location of the true suspect."

"Does he now? Where is this spot?"

"A cemetery."

"You're kidding me."

"I'm not."

"Ok. What cemetery?"

"He didn't say."

"And you believe him?"

"He only gave a small detail."

"Like what? Find the cemetery where the bodies raise up from the dead?"

"Not exactly. Said the cemetery where the suspect is presenting a form of eeriness."

"You're joking right now. Please tell me you're joking?"

"Afraid not.

Lewis nodded, glaring at the interrogation room. He saw Yana and she moved to the side, revealing Waid for Lewis to get a look at him. Lewis stared, seeing Waid holding up the calculator.

"What's with the calculator?"

"It goes with his name."

Lewis silenced himself and turned away.

"Let's just find this cemetery." Lewis said.

"Agreed."

While Cole and Lewis headed out to every cemetery they could find in searching for the eerie one, another detective had arrived at the office. Chris Harper. The chief contacted him in helping Detective Yana with their part of the case.

Cassandra traveled out into the wilderness after receiving another word from Morhana about a spiritual occurrence deep in the forest. Cassandra stopped her car and walked into the wilderness just as the sun was setting. With the surroundings growing dim, Cassandra took out her flashlight and searched the area. Unsure of what to find, she pulled out what appeared to be a compass. However, this compass was glowing. The colors reminded her of the northern lights only instead of the green, there was violet.

"Now, where do I go?" She asked herself.

She continued walking in the wilderness as the snow fell over her. The ground was covered in snow as she began to pick up her feet to continue walking. Nightfall had come and Cassandra was still in the forest. She looked around, seeing nothing but trees and snow. With that moment, she heard a loud breathing sound coming from the trees.

"Who's here?"

The breathing continued, followed by rustling snow and low thumping sounds. The thumping could be felt under Cassandra's feet and they began to grow in volume and feel. The compass ringed loudly as the violet colors transformed into a dark red. Right at the moment, the breathing had ceased. Except for the one huff of breath which was behind Cassandra. She slowly turned to see the source of the breathing and found herself staring at a colossal figure. She could only point out the horns, the legs, and the eyes.

"What are you?!" she screamed.

Cassandra started stepping back as the figure huffed once more and dragged its feet into the snow. Its breath could be seen through the chilly air. With the moonlight, Cassandra was able to get a better look at the figure. Seeing it's a hybrid of a man and a bull.

"A minotaur." She said softly.

The beast began to charge toward Cassandra and before the horns could touch her, the beast was pulled back by a larger entity hidden in the shadows of the trees. Cassandra moved herself to see and she saw the minotaur struggling to get away from the Mutant-Thing. The Mutant-Thing was covered in snow and was nearly camouflaged in the wilderness. The minotaur went to fight back, punching the Mutant-Thing with his man-like hands and rammed the Mutant-Thing with its horns. The horns went for another strike and the Mutant-Thing grabbed them, breaking one of the horns. The minotaur screeched as it trampled away. Cassandra stood still, gazing at the Mutant-Thing in awe.

"Who are you?" she asked.

"Leave this place." The Mutant-Thing commanded.

"Leave?"

"Go now."

"But, what should I tell everyone else? You saved me."

"Leave." The Mutant-Thing said once more.

Cassandra took in the words ad nodded before returning to her vehicle. Once she entered her car, she looked back at the trees, not seeing the Mutant-Thing. She sighed as she drove away from the woods.

V

<u>HYBRID OF MAN AND BEAST</u>

While Cole and Lewis were away from the office, Detective Harper had met with Yana and they began to question another suspect, who dimmed himself only a witness. The man claimed to have the ability to control the weather and brought with him a suit. A sleek uniform decorated in the colors of silver and red. He stated it was made of nanofibers, which the detectives quickly tossed away. He also included goggles and a wristwatch. Although, the wristwatch was not an actual watch. It was the source of his theory to controlling the weather.

"How is this possible?" Harper asked.

"Simple! You put on the suit and the watch. Afterwards, you have the power to change the weather to whatever you so desire."

"We're not buying this guy's games." Yana said. "He can't be a witness."

"Listen, Mr. Marston."

"Um. Mr. James Marston. But, call me… The Climate Control."

Yana looked around and shook her head in shame and let out a depressing sigh. She fanned away Marston as she approached the door.

"I'm done for the night." Yana said, exiting the room.
"Can I go now?" Marston asked.
"No." Harper replied boldly.

74

Dr. Grint continued working in his lab as the snowfall began to increase. The chill in the air didn't faze the scientist or interfere with his work. It in truth, enhanced it. Grint continued working more during the snowfall than the early hours where there was only calmness in the air. Grint stood over a large vertical table. Pulling tubes and cords from the surrounding walls, attaching them to a larger object on the table. Grint walked over to the desk and flipped a switch. There, a peculiar fluid moved though the tubes and entered the large object. The object itself appeared as what some would call a cocoon.

"In just a matter of sure moments. My work will be finished. A creation between man and beast."

VI

A VISITANT STRANGER

Cassandra returned to her apartment. She laid down her belongings on the table and as she walked toward the bedroom, she flipped the light switch and the lights flickered. Strange to her as the lights worked well earlier in the day. Unsure as to the occurrence, she flipped the switch again, turning the lights off. Flipping it again, the lights turned on and she paused herself, backing up against the closet door.

"Who are you?" She asked.

"Do not fear me, Cassandra Day." The visitor spoke. "I am here on your behalf."

"But, how did you get in here?"

"I have my ways. Ways beyond the borders of the natural realm."

"Are you a ghost?"

"I am not. I am known across the realms as the Visitant Outlander."

"I've never heard of you."

"Many have not. Few have encountered me. Now, you are one of the few."

"Why are you here?" Cassandra asked. "Why visit me?"

"Because of your reaction to the Mutant-Thing."

Cassandra relaxed herself, walking out of the bedroom to the living room of the apartment. Within seconds, the Visitant Outlander was standing in the living room, startling her. He understood and gave a slight nod, showing his understanding.

"You know of the creature?"

"I do. I was around before it even existed."

"How old are you exactly?"

"Far older than the world you see today."

Cassandra nodded.

"The creature did not attack me." Cassandra noted. "I'm not sure why. It looked like it was trying to save me."

"The Mutant-Thing did not harm you because you have not been tainted."

Cassandra paused, glaring at the Outlander.

"What do you mean?"

"You are a virgin. The Mutant-Thing cannot harm a woman who has not yet been married. It's a balance of nature."

"So, why come to me?"

"To tell you you're in danger if you continue down this path."

"It's my work. My job is to find out who's responsible for the murders."

"And what have you come to?"

"I believe there's something supernatural happening here. It explains you standing in my apartment right now, doesn't it?"

"Does it?"

"How can I know?"

"You spoke with Morhana earlier."

"Yes. She seemed to know something others did not."

"She knows more than she's letting you on."

"What do you mean?"

"Morhana is a witch. As you are already aware. Yet, you do not know her place within the confinement of this world. Morhana is currently hiding from others beyond even her control."

"I'm not getting what you're saying? Who's beyond her control?"

"Powerful entities outside of the borders of humanity."

"I have to ask. Are they responsible for the murders?"

"No."

"So, since you know so much." Cassandra said. "Then, you know who the murderer is."

Outlander grinned.

"I know who's responsible."

Cassandra approached Outlander, seeing his height was far over her own. She sighed, taking a step back. She sighed.

"Can you tell me who it is?"

"You've already met him."

"Him?" Cassandra jolted. "Who?"

"Take the moment to meditate. Then, it will come to you."

Cassandra walked over to the table, grabbing her journal. she turned back and the Outlander was gone. Without a noise or sudden movements.

"And he's gone."

Cole and Lewis traveled across the regions of Winnipeg to the cemeteries. The trail led them toward the last cemetery. They parked the car and walked through the gated entrance and out into the field of graves. Lewis held out the flashlight to keep a look around. Cole walked slowly behind him with no flashlight. He only wanted the moonlight to show him around. The field was covered in snow which annoyed Lewis.

"Didn't expect this much snow out here."

"Snow was said in the forecast."

"Oh good. What's the name of this one?" Lewis asked.

"Elmwood."

"Elmwood, huh. The place looks closed."

"Well, to the public it is."

"And us?"

"We're here on business."

"Good point. The place is giving me the creeps."

"You just now noticed?"

"Yeah. You don't appear to be a little shaken up out here."

"Because I sensed it as we drove up here."

Lewis scoffed, shaking his head.

"Figures."

Walking through the cemetery, they looked at all the headstones, seeing the names of the deceased. Lewis continued searching around as Cole showed his respect to the graves around him. While walking, Lewis stopped in front of one headstone, seeing no inscriptions. The grave was also set next to a tree.

"Hey, Cole. Come look at this."

Cole walked over, seeing the unnamed headstone. His eyes focused and he sighed. Lewis was uncertain. Waving the flashlight around the headstone and the grave. Lewis spotted several spots of fresh dirt in the mix with the snow. The appearance seemed to indicate to Lewis the grave had been buried in recent hours.

"I wonder who's grave this is?" Lewis said.

"Don't." Cole said. "Don't bother with it."

"Why the hell not? This don't seem strange to you?"

"Oh, it does. Very."

While Cole stepped back from the grave, Lewis bent down, moving the snow from the grave, finding the dirt. Lewis grinned as he started wiping the dirt. Cole went to grab him and a decaying hand arose from the dirt, snatching Lewis by his tie.

"The fuck is this?!" Lewis screamed.

"Move back!" Cole yelled. "Move back!"

Cole grabbed Lewis and pulled him from the hold. They moved back with their guns in hand as the hand rose from the ground, exposing the body. The figure which came out of the grave looked decayed from head to toe. Lewis was terrified and Cole was intrigued. The figure was dead, but it's behavior was as if it was not dead.

"There's zombies now." Lewis asked.

"How would I know." Cole replied.

"I wasn't asking."

Lewis fired a shot and it had no effect. The deceased one screeched and behind the detectives emerged a disembodied spirit, which was visible to their eyes. The spirit grabbed the deceased one and returned it into the grave, sealing the dirt over its body without a fight.

"What is that?" Lewis wondered.

The spirit turned back toward the detectives and nodded. Lewis and Cole were unsettled. Both frozen in place and hesitant to move for their firearms.

"What are you?!" Lewis yelled. "The hell are you here for?!"

"I saved your lives."

"Saved our lives?" Cole said. "How and why?"

"You were trespassing on the grave of the Restoration Man. I am the one who keeps those such as himself in line to the natural order."

Lewis waved his finger back and forth between the spirit and the grave. The sudden appearance of a spirit made Lewis feel unsure to his surroundings this night. The snow and the chilly air did not help. The spirit kept its composure in a unusual way toward the detectives. Cole only stared in a creepy awe of the spirit. Questions began to linger in his mind. What should he ask and what does the spirit know.

"Restoration Man?..." Lewis said while catching his breath. "You're dead too or something?"

"That man is called the Restoration Man?" Cole asked.

"He is. He cannot be killed. If he's every brutally harmed, he will rise once more. It is his nature and his curse."

"And you're not like him?" Lewis questioned. "Like, if I were to shoot you, the round wouldn't harm you?"

"How can it? My body isn't made of this natural world such as yourselves."

"But, you were once human?" Cole said. "Weren't you?"

"I was once alive like the two of you. Now, I am a spirit who wanders and protects."

"Your accent." Cole said. "You're not from around here are you?"

"I was once known as Robert Shaw. Now, I am only known as the Ghost of England."

"You're from England?" Lewis asked. "Like London, England?"

"I am."

"So, why are you here in Canada? In Winnipeg?"

"I was summoned here by the Restoration Man's rise. You interrupted his sleep."

"The dead don't sleep." Lewis replied. "He was, is dead."

"I see you're not keen on the workings of the land beyond. No matter, leave this cemetery and continue on with your case."

"You know we're on a case?" Cole said intriguingly.

"Yes. Who you're searching for is not here. In fact, you've already spoken to them."

"What are you saying, ghost?" Lewis asked.

"Go and the answer will come."

The Ghost of England disappeared into the night sky. Lewis placed his gun back into his holster while looking at Cole, who was only focused on the sky. Trying to see if he could catch a glimpse of The Ghost.

"You see all this shit?" Lewis asked.

"Yes."

"And you're not bothered by any of this? Anything we've encountered these past hours?"

"Not really."

Lewis shook his head and shivered from the cold air.

"I'm going home." Lewis said. "I need some sleep after all of this nonsense."

VII

THE TRUTH OF ACTIONS

The following morning after the events which transpired, Lewis and Cole returned to the office and as they walked in, Cassandra was standing at the chief's door talking to him. Lewis pointed.

"That must be the reporter he told us about."

"Who else could it be."

Walking past them was Yana and Harper. They moved with haste toward the interrogation room. Cole wondered what the purpose for their speed was. He approached the interrogation room door as it closed and inside he saw the two detectives questioning another possible suspect. Only this time, the supposed suspect was very active and seemed a little shaken. Lewis walked over next to Cole, glancing through the door window.

"Another one?" Lewis asked.

"No. This one's different. He's not responsible."

"After what we were told, of course not."

Lewis rubbed his chin, trying to get a clear hearing through the window. He stopped himself and sighed.

"You wanna see what they're talking about?" Lewis asked.

"After you."

Lewis opened the door as Yana and Harper turned around to see him and Cole walking in with Cole shutting the door stealthy, even though the other detectives can see him. Harper stood up, pointing toward them and giving a glance at the door. He scoffed with a smirk.

"Trying to be ninjetic?"

"Ninjetic?" Lewis said. "Is that a word?"

"It is now. I'm not sure why you two are in here. But, this is myself and Yana's operation at the moment."

"Well, we came in to see if you needed a few extra hands." Lewis replied.

"Extra hands aren't needed if you're just questioning a potential suspect."

"I'm not a suspect!" The man said at the table. "I'm a witness. A clear witness."

"A witness to what?" Cole asked. "What did you see?"

"I saw everything."

"What's your name, son?" Lewis asked.

"Pablo Lopez."

"Pablo." Harper said. "Tell us how you know everything?"

"I worked for the government for a time. Saw some things they were operating on and I couldn't partake in it no longer."

"What kind of stuff?" Lewis asked. "Give us something."

"I worked in the scientific field. I saw tests. All kinds of tests."

"You're gonna have to give us more than just tests, Pablo." Harper said.

"I agree." Cole added.

"Ok. I was working alongside another scientist. His last

name started with a G. But his first name was Larry. That I remember. we worked on hybridizations."

"Hybridization?" Cole said. "What kind of hybrids were you working on?"

"The mixing of man and beast with certain elements of nature."

"Like plants?" Lewis asked.

"Yes."

"Wait." Cole said. "You said the scientist you worked with was named Larry?"

"Yes. I can't remember his last name. We usually went by first-name basis in the lab. It was his protocol."

"You know a scientist named Larry?" Yana asked Cole.

"In a matter."

Cole turned toward Lewis and Lewis nodded. The two exited the interrogation room, standing by the door. Lewis gazed around at the other officers walking past them through the lobby area.

"You know who he's talking about." Cole said.

"Yes. I know. What are we going to do about him?"

"We could pay him another visit."

"You think he would allow us back in after our first visit? The bastard didn't even pay us any attention. Why would he listen to us now?"

"Because we have evidence of his involvement."

"The kid never said he was involved."

"But the Ghost did." Cole noted.

"The Ghost didn't give us much to go on."

"He gave us enough. Dr. Grint is the killer."

"So, what's our next move?"

"Let's dig up whatever we can on Dr. Grint. Find out what he's been a part of."

"And how are we going to do that while working on this case?"

Cole looked over to the chief's door, seeing Cassandra. Lewis noticed and nodded.

"Let's see."

They approached Cassandra as she was finishing up her conversation with the chief. She turned around just as they stood next to her. Lewis extended his hand.

"Detective Lewis Knight. We haven't had the chance of meeting."

"Oh. You're the two detectives working on the same case."

"We are. I'm Detective Cole Yeager."

"Nice to meet the both of you. So, what have you uncovered so far?"

"We believe Dr. Grint is the killer."

"How did you come up with that conclusion?"

"The two other detectives are speaking with a witness in the other room." Lewis said. "He told us the scientist he worked with is named Larry. Dr. Grint's first name is Larry."

Cassandra nodded.

"Then, what's your next move? Interrogate Dr. Grint into admitting to murder?"

"No. we need to check Dr. Grint's background to make sure the witness is telling us the truth."

"And you want me to dig into the history books?"

"You read out mind." Lewis grinned.

"Very well, I'll go see what I can find. Once, I do, we'll meet up back here then?"

"Sure." Cole replied.

Cassandra headed out and went into extensive research. Gong as far as to travel to libraries to research the scientific history surrounding Grint as his name was featured across various articles all speaking on hybridization and the proposed future of humanity becoming more than just human. Cassandra found little, but nothing with much weight. After she traveled to laboratories settled across Winnipeg and discovered old files and documents which were labeled *confidential* by the government. Inside the files were photos and documents speaking of a hybridization project. The names she read on the files were many, only one stood out in bold."

"Timothy Fegan?" Cassandra said.

The file documented Timothy Fegan being the test subject for the hybridization project overseen by Grint and his team. In the file was an image of the team and Pablo was present, only referred to as an intern. The remaining files detailed Fegan's disappearance from the public eye and the project went into darkness. There was nothing else available to the public concerning the project or Fegan. The team was broken up and Grunt was fired from the project and went into hiding, presumably finishing up the project on his own. Cassandra placed the file in her bag as she left the laboratory.

VIII

<u>THE HIDDEN BEAST</u>

Cassandra returned to the office where Cole and Lewis waited. She approached them hastily, pulling out he file she found. Lewis grabbed it and opened it, seeing the details. Cole glanced over, seeing the black and white photographs.

"Where did you find this?" Cole asked/

"I did some looking around. Came across one of the old labs in the city and discovered this in the archives."

"This states Dr. Grint was involved in some crazy shit." Lewis said. "Does anyone else know about this?"

"If they do, they're keeping themselves very quiet and very hard to find."

"Grint isn't hard to find." Cole added. "We should go and ask them about this."

"Yeah."

"Wait." Cassandra said. "I'm going along too."

Lewis scoffed with a short laugh.

"Look, I know you want to come with us and record all of it, but, this might get deadly and we don't need someone caught in the crossfire."

"You saw what was in that file. There's not telling what Grint is working on right now. He could be finishing what he started. You'll need all the hands you can get."

"She has a point." Cole said.

"Don't help her." Lewis grunted. "Very well. Just do not get in our way."

"You'll barely know I'm even there."

They went toward the door as Yana and Harper were walking back inside. They stopped, seeing them. Yana was uncertain of their motives and called out to them. Cole turned back, nodding to Lewis and Cassandra to head to the car.

"Where are you three going?"

"We have a lead on the case. We're going to pay someone a visit."

"And that's why the reporter is tagging along?" Harper questioned. "You sure she can take care of herself?"

"We'll see once we're there."

The three left the office and made their return to Grint's laboratory. Immediately, they noticed a strangeness in the air as soon as they pulled up. Exiting the vehicle, Cassandra looked around in the air, Lewis noticed her movements and glanced upward.

"What is it?" Lewis wondered.

"There's something in the air. Something's watching us."

"Like what?"

"I'm not sure."

"What does it feel like?" Cole asked.

"It feels… it feels evil."

The energy in the air communicated with Cassandra, turning her attention toward the door of the lab. She pointed as Cole and Lewis looked in the direction. With a nod, she knew for certain the energy was coming from within the lab. Lewis nodded and reached for his gun, rushing toward the door and kicking it open. Cole and Lewis had their guns up, aimed at Grint while Cassandra remained behind them. Grint was working on the table as he was prior.

"Put the tool down." Lewis said. "Turn around."

Grint stopped, holding the tool in his hand. He turned around slowly to see the detectives. What Grint held in his hand was a large kitchen knife. Lewis' eyes enlarged as he stepped forward with one foot. Cole glanced at Lewis' movement.

"Put the knife down." Lewis said.

"What's going on here?" Grint asked.

"The knife." Cole said. "Put it down."

"But, why? What's happening here?"

"Put the fucking knife down!" Lewis screamed. "I won't ask again!"

Grint nodded. Putting the knife down on the table. Lewis sighed. Cole remained steady and Cassandra was silent.

"We know what you were working on." Cole said. "The secret experiments."

"Experiments?"

"Yeah." Lewis said. "Some shit called hybridization."

Grint grinned.

"What's funny?" Cole asked.

"I guess it would've came out sooner or later."

"What came out?" Lewis questioned. "The hell you talking about?"

"My work. It has never ceased."

"And I assume that's what you've been doing here ever

since?" Cole said. "Trying to complete your work?"

"Of course."

"So, you're the cause of the murders?" Lewis questioned.

"They were only failed subjects to the cause."

"You admit you killed them?" Cole asked. "And the animals too?"

"All subjects which failed to endure the trials of perfection."

"You're sick." Lewis said. "A sick man."

"Sick is just a term used by the illiterate to describe brilliance."

Grint backed up against the table, putting his hand atop a control panel. Lewis jerked his gun forward.

"Step away from the table!"

"Sure. Sure."

As Grint moved, his finger pressed the black button on the panel and the lights flickered. Distracting the detectives, Grint made a run for it deeper into the lab. Lewis noticed and ran after him. Cole went to follow, telling Cassandra to remain at the door just in case. Cole ran and reached Lewis, who had stopped in his steps, seeing Grint standing at the vertical table with the cocoon.

"What is that?" Cole said.

"My ultimate creation. I believe it's time to be awakened."

"Do not make a move." Lewis said. "One more move and I will shoot you."

"Go ahead and do your work. I will do mine."

Grint took a step toward the table and Lewis fired a shot, Grint ducked as he pressed a green button on the table, in which separated the tubes from the cocoon and from there, the cocoon began to shiver, moving with intensity as Grint stepped back against the wall. Lewis and Cole were uncertain of what to do, so they aimed their guns toward the cocoon. After a minute, the cocoon busted open and from it arose a towering figure. Its figure appeared humanoid, but its hands, feet, face, and eyes appeared very much like an animal. A mixture of a human, a bear, and a wolf. The creature screeched and it was loud to the point it reached Cassandra.

"What was that?" She questioned.

Grint applauded the creature, standing beside it. The creature glared over toward Grint, who nodded with a smile.

"You are reborn!" Grint said. "No more are you Timothy Fegan!"

"Fegan?" Cole said.

"Yeah." Lewis replied. "The man from the file."

"You are now known as The Hybrid!"

Lewis and Cole began firing at the Hybrid as Grint moved out of the way. The bullets did no harm to the Hybrid's body as the hair was dense enough to preserve the body from gunfire. The Hybrid humped down from the table, swiping the detectives out of its path and bolted into the wall, crashing through as it ran to the outside. Cassandra looked around, hearing the explosion and when she walked over to the side of the lab, she saw the Hybrid, running on all fours into the wilderness.

"He's done it."

While the Hybrid ran through the wilderness, seemly making its way toward Winnipeg, the Mutant-Thing arose from the dirt in a far region, sensing the Hybrid's essence and hearing the screeching. From there, the Mutant-Thing melted into the dirt and moved with speed, following the path of the Hybrid.

IX

THE WAYS OF SCIENCE AND MYSTERY

The Hybrid made its entrance in the downtown region of Winnipeg, frightening the civilians as it began hurling vehicles into the air, slamming its arms into the pavement, shaking the ground. The police had arrived and exited their vehicles. Their firearms aimed and ready. The Hybrid saw them and showed a grim smile before charging toward them. The rounds went off, firing at all ranges toward the Hybrid. The bullets did nothing as they bounced off the fur. The Hybrid moved with a much greater speed, tackling the officers against their own vehicles, crashing them into one another. The Hybrid screeched and went further into the city.

Back at the lab, Lewis and Cole followed Grint as he made his escape into the basement of the laboratory. Cassandra entered the operating room, seeing the vertical table and the massive hole in the wall.

"Where did they go?"

She looked around and turned her attention forward. She moved and glanced over to her left, seeing a portion of the brick wall was moved to the side, revealing a set of stairs going down. She didn't hesitate. Figuring Lewis and Cole went down, she was going as well. Pacing herself down the stairs, she could hear faint echoes of Lewis shouting Grint's name followed by gunfire. Stepping foot on the ground, leading into a narrow hallway with water flowing on the ground, she noticed Cole standing in the distance. Moving faster, she caught up to him and he was not pleased.

"Why are you down here?"

"I saw something outside. It was massive."

"Yeah. That was Grint's experiment completed."

"The project he was working on? That was the subject?"

"Yes. That subject you saw rushing into the woods was once Timothy Fegan."

"Ok. Where's Lewis?"

"Catching up on Grint's trail. I'm here just in case the doctor makes a u-turn."

"I can help out, you know. Find a way to lure Grint out and-"

"You're better off back at the car."

"And what if Grint gets out of your sights? What then?"

"Lewis and I have it covered. Just wait back at the car. Please."

Cassandra let out a short sigh and turned back. Once she did, Lewis ran toward Cole, grabbing her focus.

"Did you find him?" Cole asked.

"This place's a maze. However, he somewhere down here."

"Then, let's find him."

Lewis looked over Cole's shoulder, seeing Cassandra. He shook his head.

"Why are you down here?"

"Trying to find you two."

"Did you see the big thing bolt out of the wall?"

"I did. It went into the forest. My guess it's going somewhere crowded."

"The city." Lewis said. "Every damn time."

"Look, we need to find Grint now. Sun's going down soon and we don't need to be out here at night."

"The hell we don't" Lewis agreed. "Let's get this over with."

While they searched for Grint in the sewer-life tunnels, they were ambushed by several dwarfish entities. They attacked with slashes to the legs before vanishing in the air. Only leaving a small echo of laughter following their attacks. Lewis looked around as the light in the tunnels were growing dim. Cole held his gun steady, and Cassandra remained at the entrance to the tunnels. In her right hand however was a glock.

"You see those things by any chance?" Lewis asked.

"Just a quick glance."

"And what did they look like? Besides elves?"

"Hobbits."

"Great. So, Grint's down here making fantasy characters come to life."

"They've always existed, Lewis. It's just they remain in hiding."

"And how do you know this?"

"History speaks of it."

Lewis nodded.

"That's good. Didn't know you were a historian as well. Must work well in your other endeavors."

"Comes and goes in favors."

"That's great. Now will any of that history shit help us find Grint or not?"

Cole stared and before he could answer, Grint jumped in front of them, holding a knife in one hand and a gun in the other. Cole and Lewis held their firearms aimed at Grint. Neither of them hesitated in their steps. Their boldness intrigued Grint to continue stepping further.

"One more fucking step and I will put your ass down!" Lewis yelled.

"This has to end one way." Grint said. "Only one of us must survive."

"Make your move." Cole said.

Grint nodded, tapping the knife on his forehead. He lunged with such speed at Lewis with the knife. Lewis fired a shot, knocking the knife from Grint's hand and Lewis snatched Grint by his lab coat and tossed him against eh brick wall, pummeling him in the face and stomach with his fists.

"Don't kill him." Cole said as he watched. "We need to bring him in."

Lewis delivered one more punch to the face before exhaling and raising himself up off Grint's body. Grint laid on the floor, giggling with blood pouring down his face. Lewis and Cole shook hands.

"We done our duty." Lewis said. "Let's bring this bastard in."

"NEVER!" Grint screamed, raising up from the floor.

Grint reached into his lab pocket and took out a taser, quickly holding it against Lewis' ribs. Shocking him as he stumbled and fell to the floor. Cole looked on, firing his gun at Grint, who moved out of its path before throwing the taser into Cole's face. Cole stumbled in his steps and Grint kicked him to the floor.

"Such fools! A scientist is always prepared!"

Grint looked down, seeing Cole's gun. He grabbed it.

"A pity I can't use my own. Seeing how it fell somewhere in this area." Grint said. "The water must've washed out elsewhere. No matter, using your own against you is a message proved just enough."

Grint aimed the gun toward Cole's forehead and a gunshot fired. Grint stared into space as he glared up toward the entrance, seeing Cassandra standing with her glock aimed. From the muzzle moved smoke and Grint had realized he was the one shot as he never had a chance to pull the trigger. Grint chucked and fell to the ground with a bullet wound in his chest. Cole snatched his gun from Grint's hand and stood up, holding his head. He went and checked on Lewis, helping him up as they exited the tunnels, returning to the car.

"What about Grint?" Cassandra asked.

"We'll tell the others and they'll pick him up. He's not going anywhere."

Lewis sat in the back seat, still shivering from the electricity as Cole drove into Winnipeg.

Once they arrived, they saw the city in distraught, civilians running in mass as gunfire sounded in the air. Lewis remained in the car as Cole and Cassandra walked out, moving through the people. They continued further before finding several officers shooting and being killed by the Hybrid.

"Oh no." Cassandra said.

"We have to do something."

"We can't face that thing."

"We have to find a way."

While they thought, the ground quaked. Shaking to the point of grabbing the Hybrid's attention. The creature stood firm as the ground in front of him arose and underneath the rising concrete and dirt was the Mutant-Thing. Its red eyes glared toward Hybrid as the Hybrid screeched, dragging its right foot into the ground.

X

<u>THE CURSE OF THE MUTANT-THING</u>

The Mutant-Thing ran and tackled the Hybrid into the ground, pulling the creature by its head and slamming it into the nearby trees. Cole and Cassandra moved to a further distance to avoid the flying debris. The Mutant-Thing walked over toward the downed Hybrid, covered in bark and leaves, which arose, slashing its claws into the Mutant-Thing's chest. Stumbling the Mutant-Thing in his steps, the Hybrid grabbed the Mutant-Thing by its throat and slammed it into the pavement and stomped its chest. The Hybrid lowered its head and screeched in the Mutant-Thing's face before the Mutant-Thing grabbed the Hybrid by its jaw and pulled it onto the concrete, swiping the Hybrid's foot from its chest and reversing the attack. Now, the Mutant-Thing stood over the Hybrid with its foot on the creature's chest.

"You… do… not… belong…" The Mutant-Thing said.

The Mutant-Thing used both hands, grabbing onto the Hybrid's head and began struggling against the creature. Cole and Cassandra watched on as they saw the Mutant-Thing using all its strength as he tore off the Hybrid's head with its blood pouring and spreading. The creature is dead

99

and the Mutant-Thing tosses the head across from Cole and Cassandra. they looked down and gazed up, seeing the Mutant-Thing's eyes on them. Cassandra nodded.

"It is done." The Mutant-Thing said, as it walked into the nearby river and evaporated away.

Afterwards, Lewis was taken to the nearby hospital and the officers had arrived at Grint's lab. They confronted him as he made it to the upper floor trying t escape. The officers had their guns on him. Grint was surrounded.

"Dr. Larry Grint, drop the gun!"

"Only one of us is making it out of here alive."

"Drop the gun!"

Grint nodded with a smirk before turning the gun on himself. News had spread the next day of Grint's suicide and everyone knew he was the one responsible for the murders. Chief Thompson thanked Cole, Lewis, and Cassandra for their help. The case of Winnipeg's mysterious murder was solved. However, the Chief handed the detectives a letter. They opened the letter, which requested for their assistance in a case surrounding a growing fear in paranoia. Cole glanced at the location of the case. He nodded.

"We going to Retropolis?"

"Might as well." Lewis said.

Cassandra had returned to her home in Vancouver and as she entered, she found a visitor sitting down in her chair next to the couch. The visitor stood up and greeted Cassandra.

"How did you get into my home?" She asked. "And why are you here?"

"My name is Doctor Donald Fortune and I am here to speak to you concerning the witch, Morhana."

"Why speak to me about her? I only questioned here concerning the case in Winnipeg."

"I know of the case and the assistance of the Mutant-Thing. I understand it and I give my gratitude for the creature's help with humanity. But, I am not here to speak to you concerning the Winnipeg case. I am here to ask you some questions."

"Why? What kind of questions?"

"Important ones that could save your life. Because something is coming and its growing fast. To put it to you simply, you're in its crosshairs."

SUMMER

ABOUT THE AUTHOR

Ty'Ron W. C. Robinson II is the author of several works of fiction. Including the *Dark Titan Universe Saga*, *The Haunted City Saga*, EverWar Universe, Symbolum Venatores, Frightened!, Instincts, and others. More information pertaining to the author and stories can be found at darktitanentertainment.com.

Twitter: @TyronRobinsonII

Twitter: @DarkTitan_
Instagram: @darktitanentertainment
Facebook: @DarkTitanEnt
Pinterest: @darktitanentertainment
YouTube: Dark Titan Entertainment